WHEN THE TRUMPETS BLOW

Shamayim
PUBLISHING

Dedicated to all the children,
young and old.
May God be glorified

~ Victor & Brittany Kirven

Published in the United States by Shamayim Publishing.

ISBN 978-1-7357770-1-6

Visit us on the Web! www.shamayimpublishing.com

It was a beautiful morning.
Twin sisters, Hannah and Ava, went outside to play when suddenly they heard a strange loud noise.

“What’s that sound?” Hannah asked
as it became louder.
“Maybe an elephant and its baby!” said Ava,
as they heard another squeakier noise.

But what was it?

"That's no elephant!" yelled Hannah.
"It's just Uncle Abe and baby Eli!"

TOOT TOOT!

“What a surprise to see you!”
said Hannah.

"It is a special day," replied Uncle Abe.
"What's so special about it, Uncle?"
questioned Ava.

“Today begins the Feast of Trumpets!”
Uncle Abe shouted.

“What is the ‘Feast of Trumpets’?”
asked Ava confused.
“Feasts are yummy to my tummy, but
who wants to eat a trumpet?”

"We won't be eating trumpets,"
laughed Uncle Abe,
"but I did bring some extra ones
for you all to play."

“You see, a long time ago, the people of Israel
gathered to blow trumpets at
the same time every year.
It was a holy day to remember and
look forward to.”

“Can you imagine?
There was no other music but just many blasts
of the trumpet.”

Uncle Abe took a deep breath and made a loud sound with his instrument.

"But Uncle Abe, why a trumpet and not a flute?" asked Ava.
"Or a saxophone?" added Hannah.
"And what was there to remember?"

"That is what God commanded," said Uncle Abe. "When the trumpets blew, perhaps the people were reminded of a time when God met them at a mountain called Sinai. The Bible says thunder roared, lightning flashed, and there was a loud trumpet blast!"

"God met them? That is amazing!" said Ava.

"Yes," uncle Abe replied, "and trumpet sounds in those days had different meanings."

"When the trumpets blew, it was a way of getting everyone's attention."

"When the trumpets blew, it could mean it was time to get up and move to a new location."

"When the trumpets blew,
it could signal a sound to prepare for
battle or declare a victory."

"Like when Joshua fought the battle of Jericho.
The trumpets blew..." said Ava,
"... and the walls came tumbling down!" Hannah
finished, as Eli crashed the tower they had built.

“When the trumpets blew, it could announce the coming of an important person, like a king.” explained Uncle Abe.

The girls blasted their trumpets,
“Make way for Prince Eli!”
“That’s it.” laughed Uncle Abe.

"There were different meanings for the trumpet sounds, but we should look forward to the greatest one of all."

"One day, an angel will shout, and the last trumpet will blow. Everyone will hear and see..."

"Jesus, the King of Kings, will come with all of heaven. We will get to meet Him on that day.
Who wants to meet the King?"
ME!
I DO!

"The Feast of Trumpets can remind us to look forward to that great day. When the trumpets blow, let us listen, knowing that one day soon, Jesus will return at that special sound."

“How amazing!”
Ava cheered.

"Now that is worth blowing a trumpet for." proclaimed Hannah.

AUTHORS' NOTES

The 'Festival' or 'Feast of Trumpets' is one of seven biblical feasts commanded by God in the Old Testament and still celebrated by many today. The 'Feast of Trumpets' is the first of the fall feasts. It occurs on the first day of the seventh month in the Hebrew calendar, usually in September. While the Bible does not give much information on the 'Feast of Trumpets,' we can see throughout scripture that trumpets and the shofar (or rams horn) had much significance then and the time to come.

As a family, we are passionate about exploring Jesus in the feast days. For the 'Feast of Trumpets' we like to celebrate and blow our own shofars at home as we are reminded of Jesus' soon return at the sound of a trumpet. We encourage you to read for yourself and let us know anything else you may learn.

No one knows the day or the hour that Christ will come back, but we have to be prepared. Love God with all your heart, soul, and strength, and be ready when the last trumpet sounds.

And the Lord spoke to Moses, saying, "Speak to the people of Israel, saying, In the seventh month, on the first day of the month, you shall observe a day of solemn rest, a memorial proclaimed with blast of trumpets, a holy convocation. You shall not do any ordinary work, and you shall present a food offering to the Lord."
~ Leviticus 23:23-25

For the Lord himself will descend from heaven with a cry of command, with the voice of an archangel, and with the sound of the trumpet of God.
~ 1 Theseslonians 4:16

ABOUT THE AUTHORS

Victor and Brittany live with their six children (five daughters and one son) in Maryland. They homeschool and have traveled as missionaries to many countries as they enjoy sharing the love of Jesus Christ.

They are dedicated to raising children in the knowledge of God's word.

CPSIA information can be obtained
at www.ICGtesting.com
Printed in the USA
LVHW070955160922
728540LV00002B/9

* 9 7 8 1 7 3 5 7 7 7 0 1 6 *